ORNAMENTS IN JADE

Arthur Machen (1863–1947) was a Welsh author best known for his works of supernatural fiction, such as *The Great God Pan* (1894), *The Three Impostors* (1895), and *The White People* (1904). He is widely considered to be one of the greatest writers of horror fiction in the English language.

ARTHUR MACHEN

ORNAMENTS IN JADE

THIS IS A SNUGGLY BOOK

This Snuggly Books edition is a reprint of that which was first published by Knopf in 1924.

ISBN: 978-1-943813-60-5

Contents

ORNAMENTS IN JADE

The Rose Garden

AND afterwards she went very softly, and opened the window and looked out. Behind her, the room was in a mystical semi-darkness; chairs and tables were hovering, ill-defined shapes; there was but the faintest illusory glitter from the talc moons in the rich Indian curtain which she had drawn across the door. The yellow silk draperies of the bed were but suggestions of colour, and the pillow and the white sheets glimmered as a white cloud in a far sky at twilight.

She turned from the dusky room, and with dewy tender eyes gazed out across the garden towards the lake. She could not rest nor lay herself down to sleep; though it was late, and half the night had passed, she could not rest. A sickle moon was slowly drawing upwards through certain filmy clouds that stretched in a long band from east to west, and a pallid light began to flow from the dark water, as if there also some vague star were rising. She looked with eyes insatiable for wonder; and she found a strange eastern effect in the bordering of reeds, in their spearlike shapes, in the liquid ebony that they shadowed, in the fine inlay of pearl and silver as the moon shone free; a bright symbol in the steadfast calm of the sky.

There were faint stirring sounds heard from the fringe of reeds, and now and then the drowsy, broken cry of the waterfowl, for they knew that the dawn was not far off. In the centre of the lake was a carved white pedestal, and on it shone a white boy, holding the double flute to his lips.

Beyond the lake the park began, and sloped gently to the verge of the wood, now but a dark cloud beneath the sickle moon. And then beyond, and farther still, undiscovered hills, grey bands of cloud, and the steep pale height of the heaven. She gazed on with her tender eyes, bathing herself, as it were, in the deep rest of the night, veiling her soul with the half-light and the half-shadow, stretching out her delicate hands into the coolness of the misty silvered air, wondering at her hands.

And then she turned from the window, and made herself a divan of cushions on the Persian carpet, and half sat, half lay there, as motionless, as ecstatic as a poet dreaming under roses, far in

Ispahan. She had gazed out, after all, to assure herself that sight and the eyes showed nothing but a glimmering veil, a gauze of curious lights and figures: that in it there was no reality nor substance. He had always told her that there was only one existence, one science, one religion, that the external world was but a variegated shadow which might either conceal or reveal the truth; and now she believed.

He had shown her that bodily rapture might be the ritual and expression of the ineffable mysteries, of the world beyond sense, that must be entered by the way of sense; and now she believed. She had never much doubted any of his words, from the moment of their meet-ing a month before. She had looked up as she sat in the arbour, and her father was walking down through the avenue of roses, bringing to her the stranger, thin and dark, with a pointed beard and melancholy eyes. He murmured something to himself as they shook hands; she heard the rich, unknown words that sounded as the echo of far music. Afterwards he had told her what those words signified:

'How say ye that I was lost?
I wandered among roses.

Can he go astray that enters the
   rose garden?
The Lover in the house of the Beloved
   is not forlorn.
I wandered among roses. How say ye
   that I was lost?'

His voice, murmuring the strange words, had persuaded her, and now she had the rapture of the perfect knowledge. She had looked out into the silvery uncertain night in order that she might experience the sense that for her these things no longer existed. She was not any more a part of the garden, or of the lake, or of the wood, or of the life that she had led hitherto. Another line that he had quoted came to her:

'The kingdom of I and We forsake
   and your home in
   annihilation make.'

It had seemed at first almost nonsense—if it had been possible for him to talk nonsense; but now she was filled and thrilled with the meaning of it. Herself was annihilated; at his bidding she had destroyed all her old feelings and emotions, her likes and dislikes, all the inherited loves and hates that her father and mother had given her; the old life had been thrown utterly away.

It grew light, and when the dawn burned she fell asleep, murmuring:

'How say ye that I was lost?'

The Turanians

THE smoke of the tinkers' camp rose a thin pale blue from the heart of the wood.

Mary had left her mother at work on 'things,' and had gone out with a pale and languid face into the hot afternoon. She had talked of walking across the fields to the Green, and of having a chat with the doctor's daughter, but she had taken the other path that crept down towards the hollow and the dark thickets of the wood.

After all, she had felt too lazy to rouse herself, to make the effort of conversation, and the sunlight scorched the path that was ruled straight from stile to stile across the brown August fields, and she could see, even from far away, how the white dust clouds were smoking on the road by the Green. She hesitated, and at last went down under the far-spreading oak-trees, by a winding way of grass that cooled her feet.

Her mother, who was very kind and good, used to talk to her sometimes on the evils of 'exaggeration,' on the necessity of avoiding phrases violently expressed, words of too fierce an energy. She remembered how she had run into the house a few days before and had called her mother to look at a rose in the garden that 'burnt like a flame.' Her mother had said the rose was very pretty, and a little later had hinted her doubts as to the wisdom of 'such very strong expressions.'

'I know, my dear Mary,' she had said, 'that in your case it isn't affectation. You really feel what you say, don't you? Yes; but is it nice to feel like that? Do you think that it's quite right, even?'

The mother had looked at the girl with a curious wistfulness, almost as if she would say something more, and sought for the fit words, but could not find them. And then she merely remarked:

'You haven't seen Alfred Moorhouse since the tennis party, have you? I must ask him to come next Tuesday; you like him?'

The daughter could not quite see the link between her fault of 'exaggeration' and the charming young barrister, but her mother's warning recurred to her as she strayed down the shadowed path, and felt the long dark grass cool and refreshing about her feet. She would not have put this sensation into words, but she thought it was as though her ankles were gently, sweetly kissed as the rich grass touched them, and her mother would have said it was not right to think such things.

And what a delight there was in the colours all about her! It was as though she walked in a green cloud; the strong sunlight was filtered through the leaves, reflected from the grass, and made all visible things, the tree-stems, the flowers, and her own hands seem new, transformed into another likeness. She had walked by the wood-path over and over again, but today it had become full of mystery and hinting, and every turn brought a surprise.

Today the mere sense of being alone under the trees was an acute secret joy, and as she went down deeper and the wood grew dark about her, she loosened her brown hair, and when the sun shone over the fallen tree she saw her hair was not brown but bronze and golden, glowing on her pure white dress.

She stayed by the well in the rock, and dared to make the dark water her mirror, looking to right and left with shy glances and listening for the rustle of parted boughs, before she would match her gold with luminous ivory. She saw wonders in a glass as she leaned over the shadowed mysterious pool, and smiled at the smiling nymph, whose lips parted as if to whisper secrets.

As she went on her way, the thin blue smoke rose from a gap in the trees, and she remembered her childish dread of 'the gipsies.' She walked a little farther, and laid herself to rest on a smooth patch of turf, and listened to the strange intonations that sounded from the camp. 'Those horrible people' she had heard the yellow folk called, but she found now a pleasure in voices that sang and, indistinctly heard, were almost chanting, with a rise and fall of notes and a wild wail, and the solemnity of unknown speech. It seemed a fit music for the unknown woodland, in harmony with the drip of the well, and the birds' sharp notes, and the rustle and hurry of the wood creatures.

She rose again and went on till she could see the red fire between the boughs; and the voices thrilled into an incantation. She longed to summon up courage, and talk to these strange woodfolk, but she was afraid to burst into the camp. So she sat down under a tree and waited, hoping that one of them might happen to come her way.

There were six or seven men, as many women, and a swarm of fantastic children, lolling and squatting about the fire, gabbling to one another in their singsong speech. They were people of curious aspect, short and squat, high-cheekboned, with dingy yellow skin and long almond eyes; only in one or two of the younger men there was a suggestion of a wild, almost faunlike grace, as of creatures who always moved between the red fire and the green leaf. Though everybody called them gipsies, they were in reality Turanian metal-workers, degenerated into wandering tinkers; their ancestors had fashioned the bronze battle-axes, and they mended pots and kettles. Mary waited under the tree, sure that she had nothing to fear, and resolved not to run away if one of them appeared.

The sun sank into a mass of clouds and the air grew close and heavy; a mist steamed up about the trees, a blue mist like the smoke of a wood-fire. A strange smiling face peered out from between the leaves, and the girl knew that her heart leapt as the young man walked towards her.

The Turanians moved their camp that night. There was a red glint, like fire, in the vast shadowy west, and then a burning paten floated up from a wild hill. A procession of weird bowed figures passed across the crimson disk, one stumbling after another in long single file, each bending down beneath his huge shapeless pack, and the children crawled last, goblinlike, fantastic.

The girl was lying in her white room, caressing a small green stone, a curious thing cut with strange devices, awful with age. She held it close to the luminous ivory, and the gold poured upon it.

She laughed for joy, and murmured and whispered to herself, asking herself questions in the bewilderment of her delight. She was afraid to say anything to her mother.

The Idealist

'DID you notice Symonds while Beever was telling that story just now?' said one clerk to the other.

'No. Why? Didn't he like it?'

The second clerk had been putting away his papers and closing his desk in a grave and business-like manner, but when Beever's story was recalled to him he began to bubble anew, tasting the relish of the tale for a second time.

'He's a fair scorcher, old Beever,' he remarked between little gasps of mirth. 'But didn't Symonds like it?'

'Like it? He looked disgusted, I can tell you. Made a face, something in this style:' and the man drew his features into a design of sour disapproval, as he gave his hat the last polish with his coatsleeve.

'Well, I'm off now,' he said. 'I want to get home

early, as there's tart for tea,' and he fashioned another grimace, an imitation of his favourite actor's favourite contortion.

'Well, goodbye,' said his friend. 'You are a hot 'un, you are. You're worse than Beever. See you on Monday. What will Symonds say?' and he shouted after him as the door swung to and fro.

Charles Symonds, who had failed to see the humour of Mr Beever's tale, had left the office a few minutes earlier and was now pacing slowly westward, mounting Fleet Street. His fellow clerk had not been much amiss in his observation. Symonds had heard the last phrases of Beever's story, and unconsciously had looked half round towards the group, angry and disgusted at their gross and stupid merriment. Beever and his friends seemed to him guilty of sacrilege; he likened them to plough-boys pawing and deriding an exquisite painted panel, blaring out their contempt and brutal ignorance. He could not control his features; in spite of himself he looked loathing at the three yahoos. He would have given anything if he could have found words and told them what he thought, but even to look displeasure was difficult. His shyness was a perpetual amusement to the other clerks, who often did little things to annoy him, and enjoyed the spectacle of Symonds inwardly raging and burning like Etna, but too hopelessly diffident to say a word. He would turn dead man's white, and grind his teeth at an insult, and pretend to join in the laugh, and pass it off as a joke. When he was a boy his mother was puzzled by him, not knowing whether he were sullen or insensible, or perhaps very good-tempered.

He climbed Fleet Street, still raw with irritation, partly from a real disgust at the profane coarseness of the clerks, and partly from a feeling that they talked so because they knew he hated such gross farces and novels. It was hideous to live and work with such foul creatures, and he glanced back fury at the City, the place of the stupid, the blatant, the intolerable.

He passed into the rush and flood of the Strand, into the full tide of a Saturday afternoon, still meditating the outrage, and constructing a cutting sentence for future use, heaping up words which should make Beever tremble. He was quite aware that he would never utter one of those biting phrases, but the pretence soothed him, and he began to remember other things. It was in late November and the clouds were already gathering for the bright solemnity of the sunset, flying to their places before the wind. They curled into fantastic shapes, high up there in the wind's whirlpool, and Symonds, looking towards the sky, was attracted by two grey writhing clouds that drew together in the west, in the far perspective of the Strand. He saw them as if they had been living creatures, noting every change and movement and transformation, till the shaking winds made them one and drove a vague form away to the south.

The curious interest he had taken in the cloud shapes had driven away the thought of the office, of the fetid talk which he so often heard. Beever and his friends ceased to exist, and Symonds escaped to his occult and private world which no one had ever divined. He lived far away down in Fulham, but he let the buses rock past him, and walked slowly, endeavouring to prolong the joys of anticipation. Almost with a visible gesture he drew himself apart, and went solitary, his eyes down-cast, and gazing not on the pavement but on certain clear imagined pictures.

He quickened his steps as he passed along the northern pavement of Leicester Square, hurrying to escape the sight of the enamelled strange spectra who were already beginning to walk and stir abroad, issuing from their caves and waiting for the gas-light. He scowled as he looked up and chanced to see on a hoarding an icon with raddled cheeks and grinning teeth, at which some young men were leering; and one was recalling this creature's great song:

'And that's the way they do it.
How d'ye fink it's done?
Oh, that's the way they do it.
Doesn't it taike the bun?'

Symonds scowled at the picture of her, remembering how Beever had voted her 'good goods,' how the boys bellowed the chorus under his windows of Saturday nights. Once he had opened the window as they passed by, and had sworn at them and cursed them, in a whisper, lest he should be overheard.

He peered curiously at the books in a Piccadilly shop; now and then when he could save a few pounds he had made purchases there, but the wares the bookseller dealt in were expensive, and he was obliged to be rather neatly dressed at the office, and he had other esoteric expenses. He had made up his mind to learn Persian and he hesitated as to whether he should turn back now, and see if he could pick up a grammar in Great Russell Street at a reasonable price. But it was growing dark, and the mists and shadows that he loved were gathering and inviting him onwards to those silent streets near the river.

When he at last diverged from the main road he made his way by a devious and eccentric track, threading an intricate maze of streets which to most people would have been dull and gloomy and devoid of interest. But to Symonds these backwaters of London were as bizarre and glowing as a cabinet of Japanese curios; he found here his delicately chased bronzes, work in jade, the flush and flame of extraordinary colours. He delayed at a corner, watching a shadow on a lighted blind, watching it fade and blacken and fade, conjecturing its secrets, inventing dialogue for this drama in Ombres Chinoises. He glanced up at another window, and saw a room vivid, in a hard yellow light of flaming gas, and lurked in the shelter of an old elm till he was perceived and the curtains were drawn hastily. On the way he had chosen, it was his fortune to pass many well-ordered decent streets, by villas detached and semi-detached, half hidden behind flowering-shrubs and evergreens. At this hour, on a Saturday in November, few were abroad, and Symonds was often able, crouching down by the fence, to peer into a lighted room, to watch persons who thought themselves utterly unobserved. As he came near to his home he went through meaner streets, and he stopped at a corner, observing two children at play, regarding them with the minute scrutiny of an entomologist at the microscope. A woman who had been out shopping crossed the road and drove the children home, and Symonds moved on, hastily, but with a long sigh of enjoyment.

His breath came quick, in gusts, as he drew out his latch-key. He lived in an old Georgian house, and he raced up the stairs, and locked the door of the great lofty room in which he lived. The evening was damp and chilly, but the sweat streamed down his face. He struck a match, and there was a strange momentary vision of the vast room, almost empty of furniture, a hollow space bordered by grave walls and the white glimmer of the corniced ceiling.

He lit a candle, opened a large box that stood in a corner, and set to work. He seemed to be fitting together some sort of lay figure; a vague hint of the human shape increased under his hands. The candle sparkled at the other end of the room, and Symonds was sweating over his task in a cavern of dark shadow. His nervous shaking fingers fumbled over that uncertain figure, and then he began to draw out incongruous monstrous things. In the dusk, white silk shimmered, laces and delicate frills hovered for a moment, as he bungled over the tying of knots, the fastening of bands. The old room grew rich, heavy, vaporous with subtle scents; the garments that were passing through his hands had been drenched with fragrance. Passion had contorted his face; he grinned stark in the candlelight.

When he had finished the work he drew it with him to the window, and lighted three more candles. In his excitement, for that night he forgot the effect of Ombres Chinoises, and those who passed and happened to look up at the white staring blind found singular matter for speculation.

Witchcraft

'RATHER left the others behind, haven't we, Miss Custance?' said the captain, looking back to the gate and the larchwood.

'I'm afraid we have, Captain Knight. I hope you don't mind very much, do you?'

'Mind? Delighted, you know. Sure this damp air isn't bad for you, Miss Custance?'

'Oh, d'you think it's damp? I like it. Ever since I can remember I've enjoyed these quiet autumn days. I won't hear of father's going anywhere else.'

'Charmin' place, the Grange. Don't wonder you like comin' down here.'

Captain Knight glanced back again and suddenly chuckled.

'I say, Miss Custance,' he said, 'I believe the whole lot's lost their way. Don't see a sign of them. Didn't we pass another path on the left?'

'Yes, and don't you remember you wanted to turn off?'

'Yes, of course. I thought it looked more possible, don't you know. That's where they must have gone. Where does it lead?'

'Oh, nowhere exactly. It dwindles and twists about a lot, and I'm afraid the ground is rather marshy.'

'You don't say so?' The captain laughed out loud. 'How awfully sick Ferris will be. He hates crossing Piccadilly if there's a bit of mud about.'

'Poor Mr Ferris!' And the two went on, picking their way on the rough path, till they came in sight of a little old cottage sunken alone in a hollow amongst the woods.

'Oh, you must come and see Mrs Wise,' said Miss Custance. 'She's such a dear old thing, I'm sure you'd fall in love with her. And she'd never forgive me if she heard afterwards that we'd passed so close without coming in. Only for five minutes, you know.'

'Certainly, Miss Custance. Is that the old lady there at the door?'

'Yes. She's always been so good to us children, and I know she'll talk of our coming to see her for months. You don't mind, do you?'

'I shall be charmed, I'm sure,' and he looked back once more to see if there were any appearance of Ferris and his party.

'Sit down, Miss Ethel, sit down, please, miss,' said the old woman when they went in. 'And please to sit down here, sir, will you be so kind?'

She dusted the chairs, and Miss Custance enquired after the rheumatism and the bronchitis, and promised to send something from the Grange. The old woman had good country manners, and spoke well, and now and then politely tried to include Captain Knight in the conversation. But all the time she was quietly looking at him.

'Yes, sir, I be a bit lonely at times,' she said when her visitors rose. 'I do miss Nathan sorely; you can hardly remember my husband, can you, Miss Ethel? But I have the Book, sir, and good friends too.'

A couple of days later Miss Custance came alone to the cottage. Her hand trembled as she knocked at the door.

'Is it done?' she asked, when the old woman appeared.

'Come in, miss,' said Mrs Wise, and she shut the door, and put up the wooden bolt. Then she crept to the hearth, and drew out something from a hiding-place in the stones.

'Look at that,' she said, showing it to the young lady. 'Isn't it a picture?'

Miss Custance took the object into her fine delicate hands, and glanced at it, and then flushed scarlet.

'How horrible!' she exclaimed. 'What did you do that for? You never told me.'

'It's the only way, miss, to get what you want.'

'It's a loathsome thing. I wonder you're not ashamed of yourself.'

'I be as much ashamed as you be, I think,' said Mrs Wise, and she leered at the pretty, shy-faced girl. Their eyes met and their eyes laughed at one another.

'Cover it up, please, Mrs Wise; I needn't look at it now, at all events. But are you sure?'

'There's never been a mishap since old Mrs Cradoc taught me, and she's been dead for sixty year and more. She used to tell of her grandmother's days when there were meetings in the wood over there.'

'And you're quite sure?'

'You do as I tell you. You must take it like this'; and the old woman whispered her instructions, and would have put out a hand in illustration, but the girl pushed it away.

'I understand now, Mrs Wise. No, don't do that. I quite see what you mean. Here's the money.'

'And whatever you do, don't you forget the ointment as I told you,' said Mrs Wise.

'I've been to read to poor old Mrs Wise,' Ethel said that evening to Captain Knight. 'She's over eighty and her eyesight is getting very bad.'

'Very good of you, Miss Custance, I'm sure,' said Captain Knight, and he moved away to the other end of the drawing-room, and began to talk to a girl in yellow, with whom he had been exchanging smiles at a distance, ever since the men came in from the dining-room.

That night, when she was alone in her room, Ethel followed Mrs Wise's instructions. She had hidden the object in a drawer, and as she drew it out, she looked about her, though the curtains were drawn close.

She forgot nothing, and when it was done she listened.

The Ceremony

FROM her childhood, from those early and misty days which began to seem unreal, she recollected the grey stone in the wood.

It was something between the pillar and the pyramid in shape, and its grey solemnity amidst the leaves and the grass shone and shone from those early years, always with some hint of wonder. She remembered how, when she was quite a little girl, she had strayed one day, on a hot afternoon, from her nurse's side, and only a little way in the wood the grey stone rose from the grass, and she cried out and ran back in panic terror.

'What a silly little girl,' the nurse had said. 'It's only the — stone.' She had quite forgotten the name that the servant had given, and she was always ashamed to ask as she grew older.

But always that hot day, that burning after-noon of her childhood when she had first looked consciously on the grey image in the wood, remained not a memory but a sensation. The wide wood swelling like the sea, the tossing of the bright boughs in the sunshine, the sweet smell of the grass and flowers, the beating of the summer wind upon her cheek, the gloom of the underglade rich, indistinct, gorgeous, significant as old tapestry; she could feel it and see it all, and the scent of it was in her nostrils. And in the midst of the picture, where the strange plants grew gross in shadow, was the old grey shape of the stone.

But there were in her mind broken remnants of another and far earlier impression. It was all uncertain, the shadow of a shadow, so vague that it might well have been a dream that had mingled with the confused waking thoughts of a little child. She did not know that she remembered, she rather remembered the memory. But again it was a summer day, and a woman, perhaps the same nurse, held her in her arms, and went through the wood. The woman carried bright flowers in one hand; the dream had in it a glow of bright red, and the perfume of cottage roses. Then she saw herself put down for a moment on the grass, and the red colour stained the grim stone, and there was nothing else—except that one night she woke up and heard the nurse sobbing.

She often used to think of the strangeness of very early life; one came, it seemed, from a dark cloud, there was a glow of light, but for a moment, and afterwards the night. It was as if one gazed at a velvet curtain, heavy, mysterious, impenetrable blackness, and then, for the twinkling of an eye, one spied through a pin-hole a storeyed town that flamed, with fire about its walls and pinnacles. And then again the folding darkness, so that sight became illusion, almost in the seeing. So to her was that earliest, doubtful vision of the grey stone, of the red colour spilled upon it, with the incongruous episode of the nursemaid, who wept at night.

But the later memory was clear; she could feel, even now, the inconsequent terror that sent her away shrieking, running to the nurse's skirts. Afterwards, through the days of girlhood, the stone had taken its place amongst the vast array of unintelligible things which haunt every child's imagination. It was part of life, to be accepted and not questioned; her elders spoke of many things which she could not understand, she opened books and was dimly amazed, and in the Bible there were many phrases which seemed strange. Indeed, she was often puzzled by her parents' conduct, by their looks at one another, by their half-words, and amongst all these problems which she hardly recognised as problems, was the grey ancient figure rising from dark grass.

Some semi-conscious impulse made her haunt the wood where shadow enshrined the stone. One thing was noticeable; that all through the summer months the passers-by dropped flowers there. Withered blossoms were always on the ground, amongst the grass, and on the stone fresh blooms constantly appeared. From the daffodil to the Michaelmas daisy there was marked the calendar of the cottage gardens, and in the winter she had seen sprays of juniper and box, mistletoe and holly. Once she had been drawn through the bushes by a red glow, as if there had been a fire in the wood, and when she came to the place, all the stone shone and all the ground about it was bright with roses.

In her eighteenth year she went one day into the wood, carrying with her a book that she was reading. She hid herself in a nook of hazel, and her soul was full of poetry, when there was a rustling, the rapping of parted boughs returning to their place. Her concealment was but a little way from the stone, and she peered through the net of boughs, and saw a girl timidly approaching. She knew her quite well; it was Annie Dolben, the daughter of a labourer, lately a promising pupil at Sunday school. Annie was a nice-mannered girl, never failing in her curtsy, wonderful for her knowledge of the Jewish Kings. Her face had taken an expression that whispered, that hinted strange things; there was a light and a glow behind the veil of flesh. And in her hand she bore lilies.

The lady hidden in hazels watched Annie come close to the grey image; for a moment her whole body palpitated with expectation, almost the sense of what was to happen dawned upon her. She watched Annie crown the stone with flowers, she watched the amazing ceremony that followed.

And yet, in spite of all her blushing shame, she herself bore blossoms to the wood a few months later. She laid white hothouse lilies upon the stone, and orchids of dying purple, and crimson exotic flowers. Having kissed the grey image with devout passion, she performed there all the antique immemorial rite.

Psychology

MR DALE, who had quiet rooms in a western part of London, was very busily occupied one day with a pencil and little scraps of paper. He would stop in the middle of his writing, of his monotonous tramp from door to window, jot down a line of hieroglyphics, and turn again to his work. At lunch he kept his instruments on the table beside him, and a little notebook accompanied him on his evening walk about the Green. Sometimes he seemed to experience a certain difficulty in the act of writing, as if the heat of shame or even incredulous surprise held his hand, but one by one the fragments of paper fell into the drawer, and a full feast awaited him at the day's close.

As he lit his pipe at dusk, he was standing by the window and looking out into the street. In the distance cab-lights flashed to and fro, up and down the hill, on the main road. Across the way he saw the long line of sober grey houses, cheerfully lit up for the most part, displaying against the night the dining-room and the evening meal. In one house, just opposite, there was brighter illumination, and the open windows showed a modest dinner-party in progress, and here and there a drawing-room on the first floor glowed ruddy, as the tall shaded lamp was lit. Everywhere Dale saw a quiet and comfortable respectability; if there were no gaiety there was no riot, and he thought himself fortunate to have got 'rooms' in so sane and meritorious a street.

The pavement was almost deserted. Now and again a servant would dart out from a side door and scurry off in the direction of the shops, returning in a few minutes in equal haste. But foot passengers were rare, and only at long intervals a stranger would drift from the highway and wander with slow speculation down Abingdon Road, as if he had passed its entrance a thousand times and had at last been piqued with curiosity and the desire of exploring the unknown. All the inhabitants of the quarter prided themselves on their quiet and seclusion, and many of them did not so much as dream that if one went far enough the road degenerated and became abominable, the

home of the hideous, the mouth of a black pur-
lieu. Indeed stories, ill and malodorous, were told
of the streets parallel, to east and west, which perhaps communicated with the terrible sink beyond,
but those who lived at the good end of Abingdon
Road knew nothing of their neighbours.

Dale leant far out of his window. The pale
London sky deepened to violet as the lamps were
lit, and in the twilight the little gardens before the
houses shone, seemed as if they grew more clear.
The golden laburnum but reflected the last bright
yellow veil that had fallen over the sky after sunset,
the white hawthorn was a gleaming splendour, the
red may a flameless fire in the dusk. From the open
window, Dale could note the increasing cheerful-
ness of the diners opposite, as the moderate cups
were filled and emptied; blinds in the higher stories brightened up and down the street when the
nurses came up with the children. A gentle breeze
that smelt of grass and woods and flowers, fanned
away the day's heat from the pavement stones,
rustled through the blossoming boughs, and sank
again, leaving the road to calm.

All the scene breathed the gentle domestic
peace of the stories; there were regular lives, dull
duties done, sober and common thoughts on every side. He felt that he needed not to listen at

the windows, for he could divine all the talk, and guess the placid and usual channels in which the conversation flowed. Here there were no spasms, nor raptures, nor the red storms of romance, but a safe rest; marriage and birth and begetting were no more here than breakfast and lunch and afternoon tea.

And then he turned away from the placid transparency of the street, and sat down before his lamp and the papers he had so studiously noted. A friend of his, an 'impossible' man named Jenyns, had been to see him the night before, and they had talked about the psychology of the novelists, discussing their insight, and the depth of their probe.

'It is all very well as far as it goes,' said Jenyns. 'Yes, it is perfectly accurate. Guardsmen do like chorus-girls, the doctor's daughter is fond of the curate, the grocer's assistant of the Baptist persuasion has sometimes religious difficulties, "smart" people no doubt think a great deal about social events and complications: the Tragic Comedians felt and wrote all that stuff, I dare say. But do you think that is all? Do you call a description of the gilt tools on the morocco here an exhaustive essay on Shakespeare?'

'But what more is there?' said Dale. "Don't you think, then, that human nature has been fairly laid open? What more?'

'Songs of the frantic lupanar; delirium of the madhouse. Not extreme wickedness, but the insensate, the unintelligible, the lunatic passion and idea, the desire that must come from some other sphere that we cannot even faintly imagine. Look for yourself; it is easy.'

Dale looked now at the ends and scraps of paper. On them he had carefully registered all the secret thoughts of the day, the crazy lusts, the senseless furies, the foul monsters that his heart had borne, the maniac phantasies that he had harboured. In every note he found a rampant madness, the equivalents in thought of mathematical absurdity, of two-sided triangles, of parallel straight lines which met.

'And we talk of absurd dreams,' he said to himself. 'And these are wilder than the wildest visions. And our sins; but these are the sins of nightmare.

'And every day,' he went on, 'we lead two lives, and the half of our soul is madness, and half heaven is lit by a black sun. I say I am a man, but who is the other that hides in me?'

Torture

'I REALLY do not know what to do with him,' said the father. 'He seems absolutely stupid.'

'Poor boy!' said his mother, 'I am afraid he is not well. He doesn't look in good health.'

'But what's the matter with him? He eats well enough; he had two helpings of meat, and two of pudding today at dinner, and a quarter of an hour afterwards he was munching some sweet stuff. His appetite's all right, you see, anyhow.'

'But he's very pale. He makes me feel anxious.'

'And he makes me feel anxious. Look at this letter from Wells, the headmaster. Here you see he says: "It seems almost impossible to get him to play games; he has had two or three thrashings, as I hear, for shirking cricket. And his form master gives me a very bad account of his work during the term, so that I fear the school is doing him little if any good." And you see, Mary, it isn't as if he were a little boy; he was fifteen last April. It's getting serious, you know.'

'What d'you think we had better do?'

'I wish I knew. Look at him here. He's only been home for a week, and you'd think he'd be in the best of spirits, enjoying himself with the squire's boys, and singing and racketing about all over the place. And you know the way he has been going on, almost from the day he came back; lounging and crawling from the house to the garden and back again, staying in bed half the day, and coming down with his eyes half open. I must insist on that being put a stop to, at all events. I shall trust to you to get him up at a proper time.'

'Very well, dear. I thought he looked so tired.'

'But he does nothing to make him tired! I wouldn't mind so much if the fellow were bookish, but you see what Wells says on that score. Why, I can't even get him to read a story-book. I declare his face is enough to make one angry. One can see he's totally devoid of any interest in anything.'

'I'm afraid he's unhappy, Robert.'

'Unhappy! A schoolboy unhappy! Well, I wish you'd see what you can do. I find it perfectly useless to talk to him myself.'

It was curious, but the father was quite right in laughing at the notion of his son's unhappiness. Harry was, in his quiet way, in the best of spirits. It was perfectly true that he hated cricket, and, the headmaster might have added, he hated other boys. He cared nothing for printed matter of any kind, whether fact or fiction, and he found Treasure Island as dull as Cicero. But all through the past term he had been pondering an idea; it had been with him in the early mornings in the dormitory, in schooltime and in playtime, and he watched with it at night, long after the other boys had gone to sleep. Before the coming of the idea he had found his existence unhappy enough. He had a puffy, unwholesome face and sandy hair, and his great wide mouth was made the subject of many jests. He was unpopular because he did not like games, and because he would not bathe unless he were flung into the water, and he was always in trouble over his lessons, which he could not understand. He burst out crying one night in the middle of preparation, and of course he would not say what was the matter. The fact was that he had been trying to extract the meaning from some weary nonsense about triangles, known by the absurd name of Euclid, and he had found it utterly impossible to learn the rabid stuff by heart.

The impossibility of it, and the hopeless cloud in his mind, and the terror of the thrashing he would get in the morning, broke him down; the 'blubbering idiot,' as they said.

Those were unhappy times, but that very night his idea came to him, and the holidays became indeed desirable, and ten times desirable. Every day and all the day he elaborated and re-elaborated his great thought, and though he was as stupid, as unpopular, and unprofitable as ever, he was no longer wretched.

When he got home at the end of term he lost no time in setting about his task. It was true that he was sleepy and heavy in the mornings, but that was because he worked till late at night. He found it impossible to do much in the day-time; his parents spied out his ways, and he knew that he was much too dull to invent lies and explanations. The day after his return his father had come across him as he slunk into a dark corner of the shrubbery with something hidden under his coat. He could only stand and look hopeless, idiotic, when an empty beer bottle was drawn forth; he could not say what he was doing or what he wanted with a green glass bottle. His father had left him, telling him not to play the fool, and he felt that he was always watched. When he took the cord from the back-kitchen one of the maids was peering after him down the passage, and his mother found him trying to bind a large log of wood to the trunk of one of the trees. She wanted to know what he was doing, and whether he could not find some more sensible amusement, and he stared at her with his heavy white face. He knew that he was under observation, and so he worked at night. The two servant girls who slept in the next room often awoke, fancying they heard a queer sort of noise, a 'chink-chink,' as one of them described the sensation, but they could not make out what it was.

And at last he was ready. He was 'loafing about' one afternoon, and he happened to meet Charlotte Emery, a little girl of twelve, the daughter of a neighbour. Harry flushed to a dull burning red.

'Come for a walk with me to the Beeches?' he said. 'I wish you would.'

'Oh, I mustn't, Harry. Mother wouldn't like it.'

'Do come. I've got a new game; grand fun.'

'Is it really? What sort of game is it?'

'I can't show you here. Just walk on towards the Beeches, and I'll follow you directly. I knew you would.'

Harry ran full tilt to the hiding-place where he had bestowed his apparatus. He soon over-took

Charlotte, and the two went off together towards the Beeches, a lonely wooded hill, a mile away. The boy's father would have been astonished if he could have seen him; Harry was glowing and burning with that dull red colour, but he laughed as he walked beside Charlotte.

When they were alone together in the wood, Charlotte said:

'Now you must show me the game. You promised.'

'I know. But you must do just as I tell you.'

'Yes, I will.'

'Even if it hurts?'

'Yes. But you wouldn't hurt me, Harry. I like you.'

The boy stared at her, gazed with his dull, fishy, light-blue eyes; his white, unwholesome face glared at her almost in terror. She was a dark girl, olive-skinned, with black eyes and black hair, and the scent of her hair had already half-intoxicated him, as they walked close together.

'You like me,' he said at last, stuttering.

'Yes, I like you very much. I love you, Harry dear. Won't you give me a kiss?' And she put her arm round his neck, round the neck of the ugly, pasty schoolboy. The leaden marks under his eyes seemed to grow darker.

He dropped the parcel that he held under one arm. It broke open and the contents fell to the ground. There were three or four fantastic instruments, ugly little knives made of green bottle-glass, clumsily set into wooden handles. He had stolen a broom for this purpose. And there were some lengths of rope, fitted with running nooses. It was the idea that he had so long cherished.

But he threw himself full length upon the grass, and burst into tears—the 'blubbering idiot.'

Midsummer

THE old farm-house on the hill flushed rose in the afterglow, and then, as the dusk began to mount from the brook, faded and yet grew brighter, its whitewashed walls gleaming as though light flowed from them, as the moon gleams when the red clouds turn to grey.

The ancient hawthorn tree at the barn-end became a tall black stem and its leaves and boughs a black mass against the pale uncertain blue of the twilight sky. Leonard looked up with a great sigh of relief. He was perched on the stile by the bridge, and as the wind fell, the ripple of the water swelled into a sweeter song, and there was no other sound to be heard. His pipe was finished, and though he knew that his rooms up at the farm looked out on the red rose and the white, he could not make up his mind to leave the view of the shimmering unearthly walls, and the melody of clear running water.

The contrast of it all with London was almost too immense, hardly realised or credible. A few hours before, and his ears seemed bursting with the terrible battle of the streets, with the clangour and jangle of great waggons thundering over the stones, with the sharp rattle of hansoms, the heavy rumble of swaying omnibuses. And during the journey his eyes still saw the thronging crowds, the turbid, furious streams of men that pushed eastward and westward, hurrying and jostling one another, wearying the brain with their constant movement, the everlasting flux and reflux of white faces. And the air, a hot smoke, a faint sick breath as though from a fever-stricken city; the sky, all grey heat that beat upon weary men, as they looked up through the cloud of dust that went before and followed them.

And now he was soothed in the deep silence and soothed by the chanting water, his eyes saw the valley melting into soft shadow, and in his nostrils was the ineffable incense of a summer night, that as a medicine allayed all the trouble and pain of body and mind. He wet his hands in the dew of the long grass and bathed his forehead, as if all the defilement and anguish of the streets should thus be washed utterly away.

He tried to analyse the scent of the night. The

green leaves that overshadowed the brook and made the water dark at noon, gave out their odour, and the deep meadow grass was fragrant, a gale of scent breathed from the huge elder-bush that lit up the vague hillside, hanging above the well. But the meadow-sweet was bursting into blossom at his feet, and ah! the wild red roses drooped down from dreamland.

At last he began to climb the hillside towards those white magic walls that had charmed him. His two rooms were at the end of the long low farm-house, and though there was a passage leading to the big kitchen, Leonard's sitting-room opened immediately on the garden, on the crimson roses. He could go and come as he pleased without disturbing the household, or as the pleasant farmer had expressed it, he had a home of his own. He entered and locked the door, and lit the two candles that stood in bright brass candlesticks on the mantelpiece. The room had a low ceiling crossed by a whitewashed beam, the walls were bulging and uneven, decked with samplers, with faded prints, and in a corner stood a glass cupboard, displaying quaint flowery china of some forgotten local pattern.

The room was as quiet, as full of peace, as the air and the night, and Leonard knew that here, at the old bureau, he would find the treasure he had been long vainly seeking. He was tired, but he did not feel inclined to go to bed. He lit his pipe again, and began to arrange his papers, and idly sat down at the bureau, thinking of the task, or rather of the delight, before him. An idea flashed suddenly into his mind, and he began to write hurriedly, in an ecstasy, afraid lest he should lose what he had so happily found.

At midnight his window was still bright on the hill, and he laid down his pen with a sigh of pleasure at the accomplished work. And now he could not go to bed; he felt he must wander into the night, and summon sleep from the velvet air, from the scent of darkness, from the dew. He gently unlocked and locked the door, and walked slowly between the Persian roses, and climbed the stone stile in the garden wall. The moon was mounting to a throne, in full splendour; below, at a little distance, there seemed the painted scene of a village, and higher, beyond the farm-house, a great wood began. And as he thought of the green retreats he had glanced at in the sunlit evening, he was filled with a longing for the wood-world at night, with a desire for its darkness, for the mystery of it beneath the moon. He followed the path he had noted, till on the wood's verge he looked back and found that the shape of the farm-house had fallen into the night and vanished.

He entered the shadow, treading softly, and let the track lead him away from the world. The night became full of whisperings, of dry murmuring noises; it seemed soon as if a stealthy host were beneath the trees, every man tracking another. Leonard quite forgot his work, and its triumph, and felt as though his soul were astray in a new dark sphere that dreams had foretold. He had come to a place remote, without form or colour, made alone of shadow and overhanging gloom. Unconsciously he wandered from the path, and for a time he fought his way through the undergrowth, struggling with interlacing boughs and brambles that dragged back his feet.

At last he got free, and found that he had penetrated into a broad avenue, piercing, it seemed, through the heart of the wood. The moon shone bright from above the tree-tops, and gave a faint green colour to the track which ascended to an open glade; a great amphitheatre amidst the trees. He was tired, and lay down in the darkness beside the turfy road, and wondered whether he had lit on some forgotten way, on some great path that the legions had trodden. And as he lay there watching, gazing at the pale moonlight, he saw a shadow advancing on the grass before him.

'A breath of wind must be stirring some bough behind me,' he thought, but in the instant a woman went by, and then the shadows and white women followed thick.

Leonard gripped hard at a stick he was carrying, and drove his nails into the flesh. He saw the farmer's daughter, the girl who had waited on him a few hours before, and behind her came girls with like faces, no doubt the quiet modest girls of the English village, of the English farm-house.

For a moment they fronted him, shameless, unabashed before one another, and then they had passed.

He had seen their smiles, he had seen their gestures, and things that he had thought the world had long forgotten.

The white writhing figures passed up towards the glade, and the boughs hid them, but he never doubted as to what he had seen.

Nature

'AND there was a broad level by the river,' Julian went on, telling the story of his holiday. 'A broad level of misty meadows, divided by low banks, between the hills and the river. They say the Roman world is lost beneath the turf, that a whole city sleeps there, gold and marble and amber all buried for ever.'

'You did not see anything?'

'No, I suppose not. I used to get up early, and go out, and leave the little modern village behind me, hidden in the hot haze. And then I would stand in the misty meadows, and watch the green turf shimmer and lighten, as the grey halo rolled away. Oh! the silence. There was no sound except the lapping of the river, the wash of the water on the reeds.

'The banks are yellow mud,' he went on, 'but in the early morning, as the sun began to shine in the mist, they pearled and grew like silver. There was a low mound that hid something, and on it an old thorn tree bent towards the east; it was a little way from the tide's brim. I stood there and saw the woods swell out of the haze in the early morning, and that white sun seemed to encompass the town with gleaming walls. If I had stayed still, I think I should have seen the glittering legion and the eagles, I should have heard the sonorous trumpets pealing from the walls.'

'I expect you have seen and heard more than that,' said his friend. 'I always told you that the earth too, and the hills, and even the old walls are a language, hard to translate.'

'And I came upon a place that made me think of that,' said Julian. 'It was far from the town; I lost my way amongst those rolling hills, and strayed by footpaths from field to wood, and all that I saw of man was here and there a blue smoke that crawled up from the earth, from the tree, it might be, or the brook, for I could see no house. I went on, always with the sense that I was following an unknown object, and, suddenly, a shape rose from forgotten dreams. An old farm-house, built of grey, silvering stones; a long barn wavering and dipping down to a black pool, pine trees overhanging the roof. It was all dim, as if it had been seen reflected in water. I went a little nearer, and I found that I was lifted free of the maze of hills. I fronted the mountain, looking across a deep broad valley, and all the year the mountain winds must blow upon the porch; they look from their deep windows and see the fleeting of the clouds and the sun, on that vast green hillside. Yellow flowers were shaking in the garden, for even on that still day the mountain wind swept across the valley. But those grey glistening walls! A light flowed from them, and they spoke of something beyond thought.

'I visited, too, the river valley, passing out to the north. The town was soon hidden behind trees, behind a curtain of Lombardy poplars, whispering of Italy, of the vine, the olive garden. The curving lane led me beneath orchards, their under-boughs dark-green, almost black, in the shadow, and the road winding between orchard and river led me into the long valley, where the forest is as a cloud upon the hill. I watched the yellow tide cease, and the water flow clear, and the breath of the wind was unearthly. It was there that I saw the burning pools.'

'You stayed for the sunset?'

'Yes, I stayed all the day within the valley. The sky was grey, but not cloudy; rather it was a glowing of silver light that made the earth seem dim and yet shining. Indeed, I say that though the sun was hidden, you would have dreamed that white moons were floating through the air, for now and again I saw the misty hillside pale and lighten, and a tree would appear suddenly in mid-forest, and glitter as if it blossomed. Yes, and in the calm meadows by the riverside there were little points of brightness, as if tongues of white fire sparkled in the grey grass.'

'And the river itself?'

'It was all the day a hieroglyphic, winding in esses beneath those haunting banks, colourless, and yet alight like all the world around. At last, in the evening, I sat down beneath a wych-elm on the slope, where I breathed the scent and knew the heavy stillness of the wood. Then a strong wind blew, high up in heaven, and the grey veil vanished. The sky was clear pale blue; in the west there was exhibited an opal burning green, and beneath a purple wall. Then, in the middle of the purple, a rent opened; there was a red glint, and red momentary rays, as if rose-hot metal were beaten and dinted on the anvil, and the sparks fled abroad. So the sun sank.

'I thought I would wait and see all the valley, the river, and the level, and the woods sink into twilight, become sombre, formless. The light went out from the river, the water paled as it flowed between the sad reeds and grasses. I heard a harsh, melancholy cry, and above, in the dusky air, a flight of great birds passed seaward in changing, hiero-glyphic order. The keen line of the hills by sunset home seemed to melt away, to become vague.

'Then I saw the sky was blossoming in the north. Rose gardens appeared there, with golden hedges, and bronze gates, and the great purple wall caught fire as it grew leaden. The earth was lit again, but with unnatural jewelled colours; the palest light was sardonyx, the darkness was amethyst. And then the valley was aflame. Fire in the wood, the fire of a sacrifice beneath the oaks. Fire in the level fields, a great burning in the north, and vehement flame to the south, above the town. And in the still river the very splendour of fire, yes, as if all precious things were cast into its furnace pools, as if gold and roses and jewels became flame.'

'And then?'

'Then, the shining of the evening star.'

'And you,' said his friend, 'perhaps without knowing, have told me the story of a wonderful and incredible passion.'

Julian stared at him, in amazement.

'You are quite right,' he said at length.

The Holy Things

THE sky was blue above Holborn, and only one little cloud, half white, half golden, floated on the wind's way from west to east. The long aisle of the street was splendid in the full light of the summer, and away in the west, where the houses seemed to meet and join, it was as a rich tabernacle, mysterious, the carven house of holy things.

A man came into the great highway from a quiet court. He had been sitting under plane-tree shade for an hour or more, his mind racked with perplexities and doubts, with the sense that all was without meaning or purpose, a tangle of senseless joys and empty sorrows. He had stirred in it and fought and striven, and now disappointment and success were alike tasteless. To struggle was weariness, to attain was weariness, to do nothing was weariness. He had felt, a little while before, that from the highest to the lowest things of life there was no choice, there was not one thing that was better than another: the savour of the cinders was no sweeter than the savour of the ashes. He had done work which some men liked and others disliked, and liking and disliking were equally tiresome to him. His poetry or his pictures or whatever it was that he worked at had utterly ceased to interest him, and he had tried to be idle, and found idleness as impossible as work. He had lost the faculty for making and he had lost the power of resting; he dozed in the day-time and started up and cried at night. Even that morning he had doubted and hesitated, wondering whether to stay indoors or to go out, sure that in either plan there was an infinite weariness and disgust.

When he at last went abroad he let the crowd push him into the quiet court, and at the same time cursed them in a low voice for doing so; he tried to persuade himself that he had meant to go somewhere else. When he sat down he desperately endeavoured to rouse himself, and as he knew that all the strong interests are egotistic, he made an effort to grow warm over the work he had done, to find a glow of satisfaction in the thought that he had accomplished something. It was nonsense; he had found out a clever trick and had made the most of it, and it was over. Besides, how would it interest him if afterwards he was praised when he was dead? And what was the use of trying to invent some new tricks? It was folly; and he ground his teeth as a new idea came into his mind and was rejected. To get drunk always made him so horribly ill, and other things were more foolish and tiresome than poesy or painting, whichever it was.

He could not even rest on the uncomfortable bench beneath the dank, stinking plane tree. A young man and a girl came up and sat next to him, and the girl said, 'Oh, isn't it beautiful today?' and then they began to jabber to one another—the blasted fools! He flung himself from the seat and went out into Holborn.

As far as one could see, there were two processions of omnibuses, cabs, and vans that went east and west and west and east. Now the long line would move on briskly, now it stopped. The horses' feet rattled and pattered on the asphalt, the wheels ground and jarred, a bicyclist wavered in and out between the serried ranks, jangling his bell. The foot passengers went to and fro on the pavement, with an endless change of unknown faces; there was an incessant hum and murmur of voices. In the safety of a blind passage an Italian whirled round the handle of his piano-organ; the sound of it swelled and sank as the traffic surged and paused, and now and then one heard the shrill voices of the children who danced and shrieked in time to the music. Close to the pavement a coster pushed his barrow, and proclaimed flowers in an odd intonation, reminding one of the Gregorian chant. The cyclist went by again with his jangling insistent bell, and a man who stood by the lamp-post set fire to his pastille ribbon, and let the faint blue smoke rise into the sun. Away in the west, where the houses seemed to meet, the play of sun-light on the haze made, as it were, golden mighty shapes that paused and advanced, and paused again.

He had viewed the scene hundreds of times, and for a long while had found it a nuisance and a weariness. But now as he walked stupidly, slowly, along the southern side of Holborn, a change fell. He did not in the least know what it was, but there seemed to be a strange air, and a new charm that soothed his mind.

When the traffic was stopped, to his soul there was a solemn hush that summoned remnants of a far-off memory. The voices of the passengers sank away, the street was endued with a grave and reverent expectation. A shop that he passed had a row of electric lamps burning above the door, and the golden glow of them in the sunlight was, he felt, significant. The grind and jar of the wheels, as the procession moved on again, gave out a chord of music, the opening of some high service that was to be done, and now, in an ecstasy, he was sure that he heard the roll and swell and triumph of the organ, and shrill sweet choristers began to sing. So the music sank and swelled and echoed in the vast aisle—in Holborn.

What could these lamps mean, burning in the bright sunlight? The music was hushed in a grave close, and in the rattle of traffic he heard the last deep sonorous notes shake against the choir walls—he had passed beyond the range of the Italian's instrument. But then a rich voice began alone, rising and falling in monotonous but awful modulations, singing a longing triumphant song, bidding the faithful lift up their hearts, be joined in heart with the Angels and Archangels, with the Thrones and Dominations. He could see no longer, he could not see the man who passed close beside him, pushing his barrow, and calling flowers.

Ah! He could not be mistaken, he was sure now. The air was blue with incense, he smelt the adorable fragrance. The time had almost come.

And then the silvery, reiterated, instant summons of a bell; and again, and again.

The tears fell from his eyes, in his weeping the tears poured a rain upon his cheeks. But he saw in the distance, in the far distance, the carven tabernacle, golden mighty figures moving slowly, imploring arms stretched forth.

There was a noise of a great shout; the choir sang in the tongue of his boyhood that he had forgotten:

SANT . . . SANT . . . SANT

Then the silvery bell tinkled anew; and again, and again. He looked and saw the Holy, White, and Shining Mysteries exhibited—in Holborn.

A PARTIAL LIST OF SNUGGLY BOOKS

CPSIA information can be obtained
at www.ICGtesting.com
Printed in the USA
BVHW032347200120
569971BV00009B/1176